STARRING SHAPES!

For Yvette, with thanks for believing in me

Text and illustrations © 2015 Tania Howells

Kids Can Press acknowledges the financial support of the Government of Ontario, through the Ontario Media Development Corporation's Ontario Book Initiative; the Ontario Arts Council; the Canada Council for the Arts; and the Government of Canada, through the CBF, for our publishing activity.

Published in Canada by	Published in the U.S. by
Kids Can Press Ltd.	Kids Can Press Ltd.
25 Dockside Drive	2250 Military Road
Toronto, ON M5A 0B5	Tonawanda, NY 14150

www.kidscanpress.com

The artwork in this book was rendered in Photoshop.
The text is set in Boudoir.

Edited by Yvette Ghione
Designed by Marie Bartholomew

This book is smyth sewn casebound.
Manufactured in Malaysia in 3/2015 by Tien Wah Press (Pte.) Ltd.

CM 15 0 9 8 7 6 5 4 3 2 1

LIBRARY AND ARCHIVES CANADA CATALOGUING IN PUBLICATION

Howells, Tania, author, illustrator
    Starring shapes! / written and illustrated by Tania Howells.
ISBN 978-1-55453-743-3 (bound)

    1. Shapes — Juvenile literature. I. Title.

QA445.5.H69 2015   j516'.15   C2014-907034-9

Kids Can Press is a Corus™ Entertainment company

STARRING SHAPES!

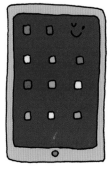

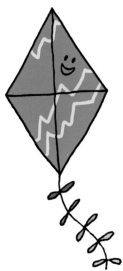

Tania Howells

Kids Can Press

The big day had finally arrived!

Everyone at Shapeston Elementary School was excited about the auditions for the upcoming school play, especially the shapes.

Triangle has already played some exciting roles.

As a traffic sign, she led the way, and she got lots of attention as a tortilla chip on the billboard near the library. Maybe you saw her strutting her stuff on that sailboat in the bay, or as the flag on your friend's bicycle?

Always the life of the party, Triangle is at her most colorful as bunting, and for Diwali one year, she and six friends made up the glittering points of a star. They lit up the night sky!

Square just wants to give acting a try.

He has many different interests. He is a natural at origami, a popular pick at quilting bees and so proud to be part of your stamp collection.

And he's always ready to help, either as a handkerchief or with your math homework. In his spare time, he loves to square dance, do crosswords and play checkers. Square is a swell guy to be around — but you probably knew that already!

Circle loves to play dress-up.

She dreams of being a gold medal at the Hula-Hoop World Championships, a famous detective's magnifying glass and the clock face on London's Big Ben. But she likes pretending to be a nursery rhyme moon best.

So far, Circle has excelled at parachute in gym class and gets lots of compliments as a perky polka dot. She always draws a crowd at the lemonade stand in the park where she works part-time as a lemon slice. Her playful personality is hard to resist!

Rectangle was born to act. He has been taking classes since he was small and has even been on TV!

He's been the cover of many popular books and magazines and taken part in art shows. Recently, he has also been busy as a tablet computer. Of course, as a jammy piece of toast, he is a very important part of breakfast.

But don't let his serious side fool you — he's always up for coloring or a game of dominoes and is lots of fun as a trampoline!

Rhombus — Diamond to her friends — has been rehearsing lines from her favorite movies to get ready for her audition.

Diamond soars high as a kite, finds her perfect fit in puzzles and dazzles in patterns — check out your uncle's argyle socks and that snake at the zoo! And she is always a favorite as shortbread at Christmas. She is as sparkly as her nickname!

She would love to be a baseball diamond and hear the crowds cheer. That would be so exciting!

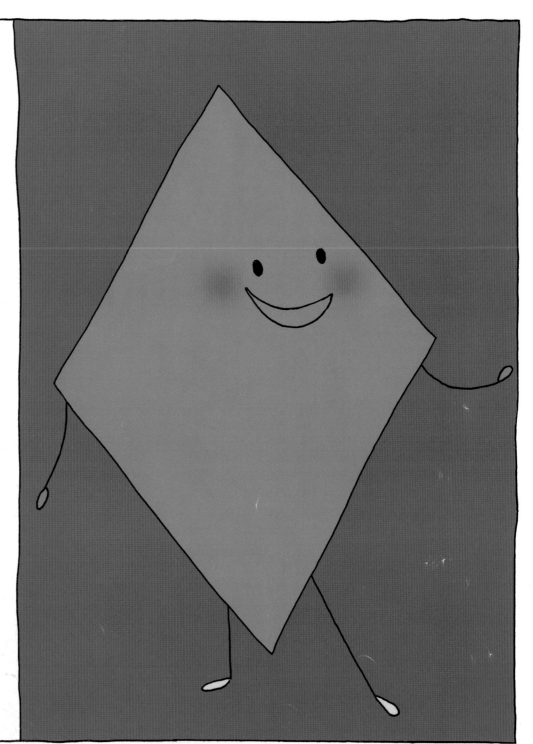

Oval thinks acting could be fun — he likes to try new things. He's a well-rounded fellow!

As a skating rink or surfboard, he is always up for an adventure any time of year! And one day he'd like to visit some of the places he's seen as a map in the classroom.

He also likes quieter activities, like making fingerprint art, stretching out by the fire as a rug for storytime and reflecting as a mirror.

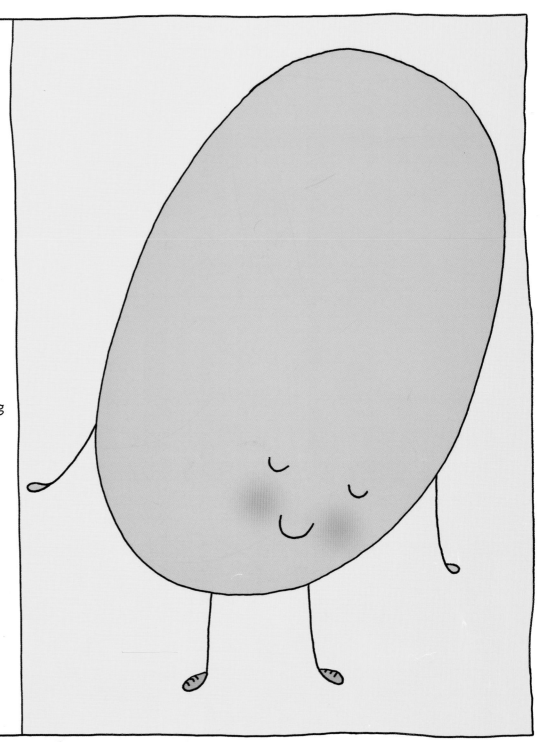

Each day after school, everyone busied themselves with
preparations for opening night.

They studied
their lines ...

Rehearsed scenes ...

Did drama exercises to develop
their acting skills ...

Made costumes ...

And helped build and paint the sets.

A few weeks later, the curtain went up. The students' production of *Hansel and Gretel* was a big hit! Everyone worked so well together. And the shapes were perfect in their roles — they are *all* stars! (Even if they aren't all star-shaped!)

Take a bow, shapes! Bravo!